GEORGE AND THE
DRAGON

CHRIS WORMELL

Mini Treasures

RED FOX

D1350925

Far, far away in the high, high mountains

in a deep, deep valley in a dark, dark cave...

there lived a mighty dragon.

He could fly higher than the clouds

and faster than all the birds.

He could burn down a forest

with a blast of his fiery breath.

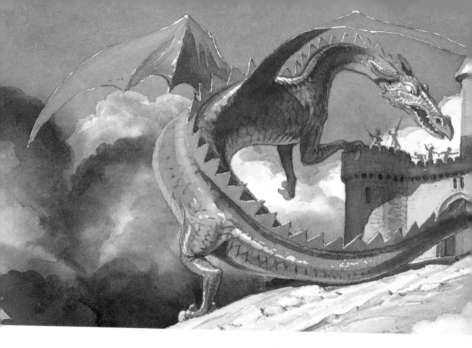

He could smash a castle wall

with a flick of his mighty tail.

And he could brush away an army

with a sweep of his monstrous wing.

There was nothing so fierce and so terrible
as the mighty dragon.

But he had a secret. A big secret, well,
actually, a very small secret...

he was terrified of mice!

Which was a pity, because that very day a
mouse moved into the cave just next door.

His name was George.

Now, George didn't much care for the cave
next door. It was cold and dark and draughty.

The previous owner had been a bat, so the fixtures and furnishings were most inconvenient.

And the nearest cheese shop was
miles and miles away.

George was feeling rather miserable.
And to make matters worse...

he had NO SUGAR for his tea!

'I know,' said George, 'I'll just pop next
door and see if I can borrow some.'
So he did.

'I say, you couldn't loan me a couple of
lumps of sugar, could you?' asked George.

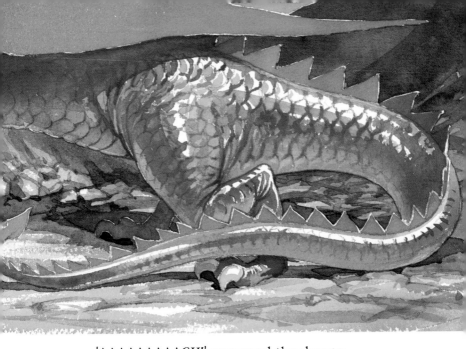

'AAAAAAAAGH!' screamed the dragon.

And fled.

'Oh, blow,' groaned George. 'No tea, then.'

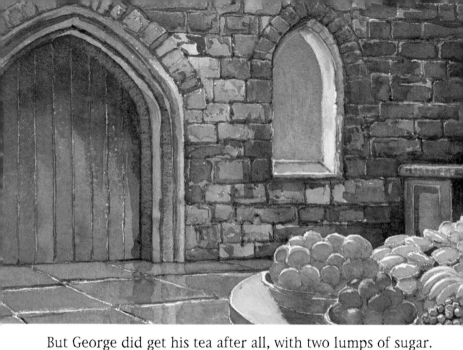

But George did get his tea after all, with two lumps of sugar.
And he got cheese, too. And nuts and berries and biscuits and

crackers and cream cheese sandwiches and jelly and
ice cream and fairy cakes with pink icing and...

a cosy little hole in the castle wall.

To John and Terry

GEORGE AND THE DRAGON
A RED FOX BOOK 978 0 099 47568 2

First published in Great Britain by Jonathan Cape 2002
an imprint of Random House Children's Books

First Red Fox Mini Treasures edition published 2004

5 7 9 10 8 6 4

Copyright © Christopher Wormell 2002

Red Fox Books are published by Random House Children's Books,
61-63 Uxbridge Road, London W5 5SA,
a division of The Random House Group Ltd,
in Australia by Random House Australia (Pty) Ltd,
20 Alfred Street, Milsons Point, Sydney, NSW 2061, Australia,
in New Zealand by Random House New Zealand Ltd,
18 Poland Road, Glenfield, Auckland 10, New Zealand,
and in South Africa by Random House (Pty) Ltd,
Endulini, 5A Jubilee Road, Parktown 2193, South Africa

THE RANDOM HOUSE GROUP Limited Reg. No. 954009

www.kidsatrandomhouse.co.uk

A CIP catalogue record for this book is available from the British Library.

Printed and bound in WKT